Tales for Telling

Leila Berg
Illustrations by Danuta Laskowska

Leila Berg brings her own very special way of story-telling to these seven delightful folk tales from five countries. Each is fully illustrated and is ideal for reading aloud at bedtime, for story-telling any time, and for young readers to try for themselves. An indication of how long each story takes to tell is given which is invaluable for those reading aloud.

*Folk tales retold by
Leila Berg*

Tales for Telling

A Magnet Book

To George Him
in loving remembrance

First published in Great Britain 1983
by Methuen Children's Books Limited
Magnet paperback edition first published 1985
by Methuen Children's Books Limited
11, New Fetter Lane, London EC4P 4EE
Text copyright © 1983 Leila Berg
Illustrations copyright © 1983
Danuta Laskowska
Printed in Great Britain
by Richard Clay (The Chaucer Press) Ltd, Bungay, Suffolk

ISBN 0 416 49280 0

This paperback is sold subject to the condition that it shall not
by way of trade or otherwise be lent, re-sold, hired out, or
otherwise circulated in any form of binding or cover other than
that in which it is published and without a similar condition
including this condition being imposed on the subsequent
purchaser.

Contents

with country of origin and approximate time for telling each story – this is very variable but a useful guide for bedtime choice.

The Girl and the Crocodile (Africa 7 minutes)	7
The Drum of the Elephants (Haiti 9 minutes)	17
Uncle Bouki's Wow (Haiti 8 minutes)	29
The Turnip-takers (Russia 28 minutes)	39
The Arguing Boy (Ireland 9 minutes)	68
Uncle Bouki Goes Fishing (Haiti 7 minutes)	79
Number Twelve (Poland 7 minutes)	89

The Girl and the Crocodile

This is a story about a promise. And this is the way *I* tell it.

Once upon a time there was a girl who was sitting on a big stone by the river, and watching the fish. And while she was watching, she felt someone was watching *her*. You know how you do?

She looked up, and there was a crocodile.

Staring. The little girl wasn't the least bit bothered. She just stared back.

'I bet you can't catch fish,' said the girl.

'Oh, easy-peasy!' said the crocodile. 'Of course I can.'

'Catch me some,' said the little girl.

'All right,' said the crocodile. 'But you'll have to give me something if I do.'

Well, the girl thought.

'I don't mind,' she said. 'On Saturday my Dad's having a birthday party, and if you come in the morning before it starts I'll give you a bottle of beer.'

'Oh, terrific!' said the crocodile. 'That's what I really do like!'

He caught a fish for the girl, and one for her Mum and one for her Dad, and she thanked him most politely like her mother had always taught her, and said, 'Don't forget now, will you? Saturday's the day,' – never thinking for a moment he'd remember. And off she went.

And the crocodile stayed in the river, crossing off his calendar every morning, and saying, 'Today's Monday.' 'Today's Tuesday.' 'Today's Wednesday.' 'Today's Thursday.' 'Today's Friday.' 'Today's Saturday. *Birthday Party*!'

And out he came, ever so excited, and swished his tail up the High Street, past the cafe, past the sweet shop, past the place where they sell cars in matchboxes, and into the little girl's street, and he knocked at the door with his tail. Frump! Frump!

The girl came to the door, because there was no one else in the house. Her Mum and Dad were out getting things for the party.

'Oh!' she said. 'Oh! I never thought . . .!'
Well, you don't, do you?

'I've come for my present,' said the crocodile.

'Oh, come in, come in,' she said, all in a fluster. 'Don't stand there on the step. I'll get into terrible trouble.'

So he came in, trying quite truly not to knock everything down with his strong tail, which was difficult because the kitchen was small.

And the girl kept saying, 'Be quiet! Oh, mind that cup!'

Then the girl got a bottle of beer from a box under the sink, and he emptied it down his throat with a plopping sound. Perlopp. Perlopp. Perlopp.

And when the last drop had gone down, he began to sing a little song.

'Crocodiles are not really bad,
Sometimes they're happy and sometimes they're sad.
Whoops!'

'Oh, do be quiet!' said the girl. 'I shall get into terrible trouble if my Mum and Dad hear you.'

'But I like singing,' said the crocodile. 'People always sing at parties. Give me some more beer.'

'There isn't any more,' she said.

'Oh, you story!' he said. 'There are hundreds of bottles under the sink. I *saw* them.'

So she gave him another bottle to keep him quiet, and he gurgled that one down too. Perlopp. Perlopp.

And he sang again.

'Crocodiles are not really bad,
Sometimes they're happy, and sometimes they're sad.
Whoops!'

'Oh for heaven's sake be *quiet!*' she said. 'We'll have everyone here in a minute, and won't they be mad at me!'

'Well, give me another bottle,' he said. So she gave him another.

And he gurgled that one down too, and sang again, beating time with his tail on the dinner-gong that the little girl's Dad had picked up at an auction last Wednesday.

'Crocodiles are not really bad,
Sometimes they're happy and sometimes they're sad.
Whoops!'

And then he wandered out of the house, dancing on his hind legs, and clapping with his front feet, and bumping into the chrysan-

themums that the girl's Dad had planted last Sunday.

And the little girl ran after him, crying, 'Oh, do be quiet! You'll get me into terrible trouble!'

And just as he went past the pond, the girl managed to push him in. But he got out, and she pushed him in again, and he got out again, and began to chase her right down the street, and past the place where you get the little cars in matchboxes, and past the sweet shop, *and* past the cafe. And he was singing,
'Crocodiles are not really bad,
Sometimes they're happy and sometimes they're sad.
Whoops!'

and she was shouting (Well you would, wouldn't you?) right down to the bottom of the hill.

Now all the Mums and Dads were coming out of their gates to go to her Dad's birthday party, because it was nearly time, you see.

And her Auntie was there. And her Auntie was very sensible and brave and quick-thinking, and she spread out her arms wide and stood right in his path, to stop him chasing the girl (whose name, by the way, was Amanda).

But it was no use. The crocodile just floppered her down with his tail, giving her a headache for weeks, and went on chasing.

But Amanda's Mum and Dad, who were just coming out of the cake shop, and all the other Mums and Dads coming out of their gates, heard the *extraordinary* noise, and came rushing up, and they stood one behind the other, and they caught the crocodile in all their hands, and they held him up in the air high above their heads, and they ran down with him to the river, and they threw him in. Flup splash!

Then they all came back to the girl, puffing a little, and her Mum and Dad said, 'Whatever were you doing with that crocodile? Now tell the truth!'

And the girl said, 'Well, you know those fishes we ate on Sunday. Well, that crocodile caught them for me, and I promised I'd give him some beer as a present.'

'*You promised him some beer!*' said all the Mums and Dads.

(And her Auntie said, 'Oh my poor head!')

And her Mum and Dad said, 'Amanda! Don't you know that we never ask crocodiles to parties!'

And all night long, when the party was finished, and all the people gone home, and the last gate shut again, they could hear the old crocodile still singing away to himself in the river, beating time with his tail on the big stone and clapping his front feet.

'*Crocodiles are not really bad,*
Sometimes they're happy and sometimes they're sad.
Whoops!'
Snip snap snover,
That story's over.

The Drum of the Elephants

This is the tale of the elephants' dance. And this is the way *I* tell it.

Once there was an old man. And he had three grown-up children still alive, all men.

One day the old man was ill. He was so ill he thought he would die.

So he sent for his children and said, 'I am ill, very ill. If I should die, how would you bury me?'

The first son said, 'Father, I am sure you will get better, and we needn't talk of dying. But if you *should* die, I will bury you in a beautiful oak coffin.'

The second son said, 'Father, I am sure you will be strong again. But if you *should* die, I will bury you in a shining brass coffin.'

The third son – whose name was Bri – said, 'Father, I am sure you will be well and happy soon. But if you *should* die, I will bury you in the great drum of the elephants.'

'The great drum of the elephants!' said his father. 'That is what I would like. Go and find the drum and get it ready.'

Bri went home to his wife and said to her, 'To make someone happy I have said a crazy thing. Where will I find the great drum of the elephants? I have never ever seen such a drum. I have never ever seen even the elephants.'

His wife said, 'You must try.'

She cut some bread, and made it into a bundle. And in the morning, when the first bird woke and sleepily called, he took his bundle and went out of the house.

He walked all day, looking for the drum of the elephants. When the day grew darker, and evening was coming, he met a blind beggar, whom a little boy was leading.

The beggar said to him, 'I am hungry. Please give me something to eat.'

Bri felt in his bundle, and took out a piece of bread and gave it to the beggar.

'If only you had eyes,' he said, 'I would ask if you had seen the elephants.'

'Even people with eyes,' said the beggar, 'have never seen the elephants.'

So Bri went on. When it was too dark to

walk further, he lay down at the side of the road, and slept. When morning came, he got up and walked again, looking and asking. But no one could tell him where the elephants were, and he couldn't find them.

As the day grew hot, he looked for a place in the shade to rest, and there he sat down. Next to him was sitting an old man, with only one foot, and a stick to lean on.

'I am hungry,' said the old man. 'Please give me some food.'

So Bri took a piece of bread from his bundle and gave it him, saying, 'If only you had two feet, I would ask if you had met the elephants.'

'Even people with two feet,' said the old man, 'have never met the elephants.'

The day grew dark again, and he looked for a place to sleep. An old man had lit a fire by the road, and called to him, saying, 'Rest here by me!'

Bri sat down and opened his bundle. There were still two pieces of bread. He gave one to the old man, and the old man ate it. Then Bri ate the other himself.

'Thank you for the third piece of bread,' said the old man. 'And thank you for the second. And thank you for the first.'

'You have made a mistake,' said Bri. 'I only gave you one piece.'

'You gave me this piece now,' said the old man, 'and now I am an old man by the fire. But when you gave me a piece earlier, I was a man with only one foot. And when you gave me a piece yesterday, I was a beggar who could not see.

So now I will tell you how to find the great drum of the elephants. Go that way, across the grassland, until you come to a huge mapou tree, the greatest tree you have ever seen, or ever will see.

That is where the elephants dance. They come there in the evening with their drum, and they dance to their drum until they are tired; and then they sleep. While they sleep, you will take the drum.'

'But will they not catch me?' said Bri.

'I am Merissier,' said the old man, 'and I am telling you what to do, because you helped me.

I will give you four nuts. If the elephants follow you, throw down a nut, saying, "Merissier is stronger than elephants!" Then you will be safe.'

In the morning, when the first bird sleepily called, Bri got up from the roadside and began to walk.

He walked the way Merissier had shown him, a long, long way, till he came to the huge tree. Then he climbed the tree and sat down at the top, among the leaves. And he waited.

As it grew dark, he saw the elephants coming. They came to the tree, and crowded round it.

'Play!' said the king of the elephants. The king's drummer began to play on the great drum, and the elephants danced.

The tree shook with their stamping, the ground trembled. The stars in the sky seemed almost shaken out of the dark, as if they would fall in showers to the ground. All night the elephants danced.

When the morning came, and the first sleepy bird called softly, they stopped their dancing, and lay down and slept.

Slowly and carefully in the early morning light, Bri climbed down. There were sleeping elephants all round as far as he could see.

The great drum lay against the tree. He took it up, with great difficulty for it was very heavy, and balanced it on his head.

Then he picked his way between the elephants, over this one's head, over that one's trunk, over that one's back, over that one's leg, still balancing the great heavy drum, until at last he was outside the huge circle. Then he began to walk fast.

But the elephants awoke. And when he was halfway across the grassland, he heard them coming after him. Quickly he threw down a nut.

'Merissier is stronger than elephants!' he said.

At once, a tall thick pine forest grew up behind him. The elephants stopped running, and began to pick their way slowly through the trees.

Bri went on, but again he heard the elephants behind him. He took out another nut, and threw it down.

'Merissier is stronger than elephants!' he called out.

And this time, a lake spread out between him and the elephants. They stopped running, and steadily began to drink up the lake, so that the ground would be dry again and they would be able to follow him.

Bri went on, but soon he heard them behind him again. He threw down a nut.

'Merissier is stronger than elephants!' he cried.

And now a sea stretched between him and the elephants. They began to drink, as before.

But a sea's water is salt, and they spat it out because they knew a whole sea of salt water would kill them.

But the king of the elephants was angry, and made them drink, till one by one they all fell dead. And only the king, who had drunk none of it, was left alive, to follow Bri over the land that was dry again.

Meanwhile, Bri had gone with the great drum to his father's house. But his father was not lying dead. He was not even ill. He was strong and well and happy, working away in the fields.

'Put the drum away,' he said. 'I don't need it today.'

So Bri laid the drum down in the garden. He got himself some supper, and then lay down to sleep.

But in his sleep he heard the king of the elephants coming, tramp, tramp, into the garden, and heard him shout, 'There is my drum!'

Immediately Bri woke, and threw the very last nut.

'Merissier is stronger than elephants!' he shouted.

The great drum broke into a thousand

pieces, and each became a little drum. And the king of the elephants broke into a thousand pieces, and each became a drummer.

And every drummer seized a drum, and began drumming, drumming, drumming. And drumming still, they marched away, all over the world.

That is why today there are drummers *everywhere*.

And that is why, too, no one has ever been buried in a drum.

Snip snap snover,
That story's over.

Uncles Bouki's Wow

Now this is a tale of market-day. And this is the way *I* tell it.

One day, Uncle Bouki went off to market.
'Now be sure you come straight back,' said Auntie Bouki. 'I don't want you wandering round, poking your nose into things that have got nothing to do with you.'
'I'll come straight back,' said Uncle Bouki.
In the market there were so many people, so much fruit heaped up on the stalls, so many vegetables spilled out on the ground. There were sounds tickling his ears and smells tickling his nose. Uncle Bouki didn't come straight back. He did wander around.
He came to an old woman with a donkey. She was sitting on the ground, resting her knobbly back against the knobbly donkey.

The donkey was eating the grass, trying to kick the old lady now and then because he didn't like her leaning against him.

And the old woman was eating ... something ... What could it be? It was yellow and juicy, and the way it ran down the old woman's chin and her tongue went searching after it, made Uncle Bouki feel very short of something.

'Excuse me. What's that you're eating?' he said. But she couldn't hear him above the noise of the market. 'What's that stuff you're eating?' he said again. No answer.

And at last she got fed up with his standing and staring, and suddenly shouted at him, 'Mind your own business and go away!' (She was having trouble enough dealing with the donkey.) So he went on a bit, feeling even more short of something.

At the next stall was a man. He was eating away too. Whatever it was, he was holding it in both hands, so Uncle Bouki couldn't see it. But he could tell it was crisp and juicy and sweet, from the way the man was eating it – chomping away, and sometimes stopping to pick a bit out of his teeth, then chomping away again.

Uncle Bouki just gazed. 'What's that you're eating?' he said at last. The man couldn't hear. He said nothing – just went on chomping.

Uncle Bouki coughed. 'Tell me what it's called,' he said. 'I'd like to get some for myself.'

But the man just chomped away, not hearing anything – till suddenly he got fed up with Uncle Bouki standing in front of him, staring, and he shouted, 'Go away and mind your own business!' So Uncle Bouki went away.

He saw an old man sitting on the bank, scooping something out of a bowl and stuffing it into his mouth with his fingers. A handful of something green. A handful of something orange. The juice dripped between his fingers and the man hummed away happily between mouthfuls.

'What's that you're eating?' said Uncle Bouki. 'Where can I get it?'

But the man didn't hear, not only because the noise of the market was too loud, but also because the man was very deaf even in the quietest places. He just scooped round the bowl, and put another handful in his mouth, something green again.

'Where can I get it? What's it called?' said Uncle Bouki again.

The old man could see Uncle Bouki's lips moving, even though he couldn't hear him saying anything, and as he was a polite and friendly man he smiled at Uncle Bouki before he took another handful.

This made Uncle Bouki think he was teasing him, and he felt even more short of something than ever.

'Tell me what it *is*!' he shouted, seizing the old man by his shirt.

Just at that moment the old man scooped something red into his mouth, and it was peppery, really peppery! 'Wow!' he shouted.

'Thank you,' said Uncle Bouki, letting go of him. 'I've never heard of that. I'll get some.'

The man said, 'Wow! Wow!' again and Uncle Bouki said, 'I heard you the first time. No need to shout.'

So the next stall he came to, he asked for some wow. But they just stared at him.

'Never heard of it.'

The next stall was the same.

'How much is wow?' he said.

'Never heard of it.'

Well, he walked from stall to stall, asking for wow. And first they just stared, then they began to laugh, then they *roared* with laughter.

And by now Uncle Bouki was very cross indeed, as well as hungry.

'I'll go home,' he said to himself, 'and get Auntie Bouki to cook me some.'

Now Auntie Bouki was a very fine cook, the

best cook in the village. Just as he came in at the door, she had got fed up with waiting for him, and she was putting dinner on the table.

And it was so crusty and crispy and juicy and sizzly, and the luscious smell of it curled up to Uncle Bouki's nose and tickled it so lovingly, that any other day he would have grabbed a chair and eaten it up at once.

But all the time he had been trudging home he'd been thinking 'I'll get Auntie Bouki to make wow. Wow Pie ... or Wow Tart ... or Wow Pudding ... or Wow with sweet potatoes ... or Wow with orange sauce.'

So he just grabbed the dish off the table and shouted, 'What's this rubbish! I want wow!'

And he threw it at Auntie Bouki.

At that very moment, Tiji, their little boy, came in at the door. He had smelled the dinner, you see.

But just as he came in he heard Uncle Bouki's shout, and the crash of the dish, and he turned to dash out again.

'Just a minute,' shouted Uncle Bouki, grabbing him. 'Here's some money, and here's a sack. Get me some wow! Now!'

So poor Tiji went outside. What a job, to get wow! He went next door to their neighbours, but they hadn't got any. They'd never heard of it. He tried the people on the other side. Same thing. He went up and down the village, but everyone stared and shook their head ... then began to laugh ... then *roared* with laughter.

Tiji sat down in the road, and wondered what to do. How could he go back without wow, with his father in that dreadful temper, and dinner all over the wall?

Clever Dick came along, whistling.

'Hello Tiji.'

'Hello Clever Dick.'

'What's the matter with you today?'

And Tiji told him what was the matter.

No wow.

Clever Dick listened carefully.

'I see,' he said. 'Well, you know how it is. All troubles vanish when Clever Dick comes along. Just give me that sack and the money, and Uncle Bouki will have his wow before he knows what has happened to him. Clever Dick knows how to get it.'

He was away for not much more than five minutes ... ten at the most.

When he came back he had put the prickliest leaves he could find at the bottom of the sack, and on top of them, things he had found strewn over the road after market-day – a run-over pineapple, a squashed orange, two broken yams, and one, two, three sweet potatoes that children had been kicking along for a game.

'There!' he said, handing the sack to Tiji. 'Special delivery for Uncle Bouki.'

Tiji took it in.

Uncle Bouki grabbed it from him, untwisted the top, and almost fell inside. He pulled out the run-over pineapple.

'That's not a wow! That's a pineapple!'

He pulled out the orange.

'That's not a wow! That's an orange!'

He pulled out the yams, one, two of them.

'That's not a wow! Those are yams!'

He pulled out the sweet potatoes, one, two, three of them.

'That's not a wow! Those are potatoes!'

Tiji was beginning to feel very worried indeed. He should never have listened to Clever Dick.

But just then, Uncle Bouki plunged his hand right down to the bottom of the sack, in the middle of those prickly leaves.

'Wow! Wow!' he shouted.

And Tiji skipped out of the house. He was so pleased Uncle Bouki had got what he wanted.

Snip snap snover,
That tale's over.

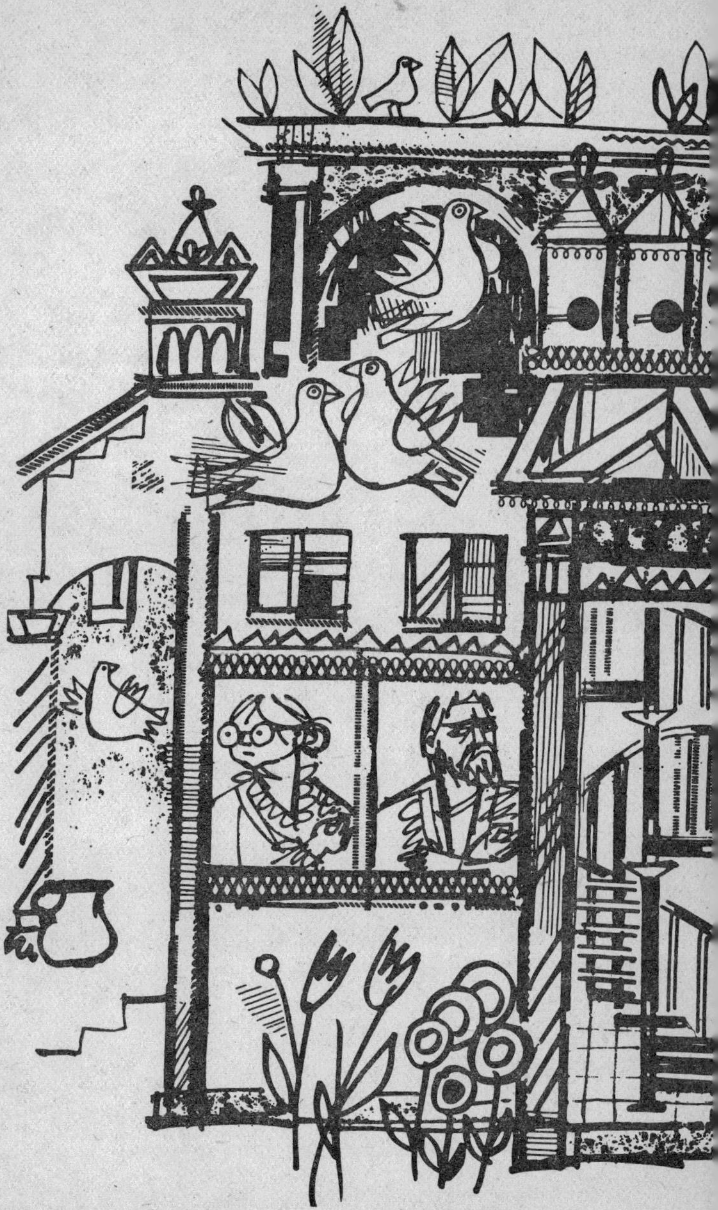

The Turnip-takers

This is a tale of a houseful of children. And this is the way *I* tell it.

There was once an old man and an old woman who lived in a house with a winding stair. The staircase went round and round, and up and up. And at the top was a high tower. And on the top of the tower was a dovecote, a birds' house, where doves walked in and out, cooing. And on the top of the dovecote was a flat roof. All this you must remember.

Now there was a large garden to this house, and it was full of rollicking flowers and almost every vegetable you can think of. But the old man was so cross and cantankerous that *he* of course wanted the only vegetable that wasn't in the garden.

'I want turnips!' he shouted. 'I want turnips with my dinner!'

'But we haven't got any turnips,' said the old woman. 'There aren't any turnips in the garden.' She did all the growing of the vegetables, and all the work, inside and out; the old man never helped her.

'Then *grow* turnips!' he shouted.

'But there's no room. The garden's full, with every other vegetable you can think of.'

'Then grow them on top of the dovecote!'

On top of the dovecote! Up and round the winding stair, up the tower, up to the dovecote, and on to the roof – grow turnips there!

'There's no soil there,' she said.

'Then put some there!' shrieked the man.

It was no use arguing. She filled a sack with soil and dragged it up and up, and round and round. The staircase was very steep, and very wobbly too, and she used both hands for hanging on, so she had to hold the bag between her teeth. As it happened, the cantankerous old man never let her eat anything but crusts – even though she did all the baking – so her teeth had grown very strong.

Well, somehow or other, she got to the tower and up to the dovecote, and emptied the soil and came down again. Up and up she went, and round and round, over and over again, with the bag bumping and swinging between her teeth, until at last there was enough soil there to plant turnip seed.

You'd think after that he'd give her a bit of a rest. But no. Every morning he made her go up and up and round and round, to see if the turnips were ready to cook. And of course they weren't. Not when she'd only just planted them.

But one morning she came down the stairs and said, 'There's a bit of green showing.' And the next day, 'They're a bit taller.'

Till at last, one morning, she tottered down from that rickety winding wobbly stair, and said, 'They're big enough now, but – '

'But what?' shouted the old man.

'But someone's been taking them.'

'Taking my turnips! My turnips!' shouted the old man. 'You get out of this house, and don't come back till you've found those turnip-takers!'

And he ran at her with a broom till she unlocked the front door – for it was still early in the morning – and hobbled out.

'But how did they get in,' she said to herself as she shuffled along, 'when the door was still locked till I opened it just now? How did they get in to take the turnips ... those turnip-takers?' But she couldn't answer that one.

She wandered past all the rollicking flowers and sensible vegetables, till she came at last to the woods. And through the dark woods she wandered, and out the other side into sunshine again.

And suddenly, there was a piercing squealing noise, a chattering twittering noise, like hundreds of starlings gathered together on rooftops, and it grew louder and louder, and shriller and shriller, till she clapped her hands over her ears and cried out 'Stop!' and squeezed her eyes tight. Just when she thought her ears would go crack, it stopped.

She opened her eyes. Straight in front of her was a little wooden hut. 'Well,' she said, 'I don't know what made that noise. And I don't know what's in that hut. But I'll have to be brave and go and see.'

So she opened the door of the hut and went inside. There was no one there. It was all neat and tidy. The plates stood on the shelves. The cups hung from the hooks. The blankets on top of the stove – for this was one of those cold countries where people sleep on the stove all night – the blankets were folded neatly. The floor was swept and clean.

But as the woman stared down at it, she thought she saw a tiny speck of something, a speck of green. She bent down to look, and it was a tiny scrap of turnip leaf!

And immediately there were gurgles of laughter, and gasps and giggles, and the blankets on top of the stove began to wriggle and heave and shake, and dozens of heads with rumpled hair and mischievous eyes poked out, and dozens of children scrambled down, more and more and more of them. And the doors of the stove opened too, and dozens more scrambled out from there, till the kitchen was full of children, every one laughing, and every one waving a turnip.

'So it was *you* stole the turnips!' cried the little old woman.

'It was us, it was us!' they shouted.

'But how did you get in, when the door was still locked?'

But they wouldn't say anything to that, just laughed more than ever, and nudged each other.

'Oh, you can laugh all right,' she said. 'But I'm the one who gets into trouble when turnips fly off in the middle of the night.'

'We'll pay for them!' they shouted, jumping up and down. 'Don't fuss – we'll pay for them.'

'Pay for them!' she said. And she couldn't help laughing herself, though goodness knows she had nothing to laugh about; but they were such lovely children, she couldn't help liking them. 'Pay for them!' she said. 'What with?'

Then they stopped laughing, and all gathered together in a little crowd and began to whisper. And again it was like hundreds of starlings whistling and murmuring in tree-tops. At last they were quiet, and one of them said to her, 'Would you like something to eat?'

'Indeed I would,' she said. 'I've been doing nothing since I got up but look for turnip-takers. I've had no breakfast.'

'Then look in the cupboard!' they all shouted. 'And take out the cloth! And spread it on the table! And shout, "*Turn inside out!*"'

She did everything they said. And when she said, '*Turn inside out!*' the tablecloth rose up in the air, and whirled about, and twisted itself, and tied a knot and untied again, and at last came down on the table and spread itself out.

And somehow or other, and somewhere or other, it had covered itself with knives and spoons and forks, and bowls with little ducks on them, and mugs with bears, and plates with daisies on them, and tureens full of hot thick soup, and dishes of roast chicken and baked fish, and huge plates of sausages and plates of chips and plates of vegetables, all golden and brown and orange and green, and some fresh brown bread, and cakes and scones, and everything you could think of for the most luscious dinner in the world.

Now the children stopped chattering and laughing. All of them, and the little old woman, picked up spoons or forks, and began to eat away.

And they ate and ate till there was nothing left on the table. Only the empty dirty plates and dishes, and the spoons and knives and forks; and there were dozens of them.

'But who does all the washing up?' said the old woman, wondering (because at home she had to do it all). The children just poked each other, and laughed.

'You can laugh,' said the old woman. 'But I know about washing up. Someone has to do it.'

'Oh don't fuss!' cried the children. 'Just tell the tablecloth to turn outside in.'

Well, the old woman wasn't surprised at anything now. She just told it.

Up jumped the tablecloth off the table with all the dirty dishes and plates and knives, spoons and forks, and it whirled through the air, it leaped and danced, and twisted and twirled, knotted and unknotted, skipped this way and skipped back again, and at last spread itself again on the table.

And somewhere, and somehow, all the dishes and plates, and the spoons, knives and forks, all the crumbs, even the brown stains of soup that were splashed all over it, had left it on its way back to the table. And now it was clean again.

'That's a beautiful tablecloth,' said the old woman wistfully.

'Take it,' shouted the children. 'Take it. And don't tell us off about the turnips any more!'

'That suits me,' said the old woman delighted. 'Thank you very, very much.' And she sang as she went home.

As soon as she opened the door the old man shouted, 'Did you find the turnip-takers?'

'Yes. Yes, I did.'

'Who were they?'

'Just a houseful of strange little children.'

'Did you beat them hard?'

'No. No, I didn't.'

'You didn't! What d'you mean, you didn't! Give them to me, and I'll beat them! I'll beat them all right. I'll teach them to take my turnips!'

'But they paid for the turnips,' she said quickly. 'They gave me this cloth. *Tablecloth, turn inside out,*' she said very fast, because the old man was getting so angry.

And the tablecloth leaped up in the air, and

when it came down on the table, somehow or other, somewhere or other, it had got itself covered again with luscious things to eat and drink.

The man said, 'Humph!' He picked up a fork, and tried the chicken. Then he had some soup ... and some fish ... some cheese ... and pudding ... and cake. But he wouldn't enjoy it. Oh no.

'What about the washing up?' he said furiously. (Not that he ever did the washing up. He always left it for the old woman.)

'That's all right,' said the old woman. '*Tablecloth, turn outside in.*'

And up went the tablecloth, with everything on it, and twirled and whirled in the air. And when it came down again, it was white and clean and smooth.

'I see!' said the man, in an angry voice. 'Well, there's nothing special about that. They had to give us something for the turnips, hadn't they? I don't see it's anything wonderful.'

The old woman said nothing. She was so dead-tired, that she fell asleep at once, just as she was, in the chair.

And immediately, the old man folded up the tablecloth, put it away in his own cupboard, and spread a different one on the table.

'Those were my turnips!' he said. 'So it's my cloth!'

First thing in the morning, he shouted to the old woman to get out of bed and climb up the stairs, to the top of the house, to the top of the tower, to the top of the dovecote, to see how the turnips were getting on.

'I will, I will,' she said, straightening up her stiff back, 'just as soon as I've had my breakfast.'

'You've no time for breakfast,' he said. 'It will take too long.'

'Not long at all,' she said, 'with our new tablecloth.' And she said, '*Tablecloth, turn inside out.*'

But nothing happened. Nothing. (You know why.)

'Ah well, that didn't last long,' she said sadly.

'Get up the stairs,' said the old man, 'and see to the turnips.'

So up she went, up the wobbly stair, to look at the turnips. She took one look, and another look. Then she counted them. And then she came down the stairs again.

'Are they growing all right?' said the old man.

'Very well indeed,' she said. 'But I'm afraid some of them – well, a lot of them – have been stolen away.'

'Stolen away!' he shouted. 'My turnips! You take a stick and find those turnip-takers!'

So she unlocked the door, and hobbled out, past the rollicking flowers and the sensible vegetables, and through the dark wood. And there on the other side was the little hut. And there was the noise, the chatter, the chirruping, the squealing, as if every bird in the world had settled in one tree.

Immediately, the door opened, and dozens and dozens of little children came skipping out to meet her. They took her hand, and they tugged her skirt, and they put their arms round her and squeezed her and pulled her. And every one, every single one, had a turnip, and showed it to the old woman, and laughed and gurgled as if it was the funniest joke in the world.

'I knew it was you again,' said the old woman.

'Of course it was us,' they laughed. 'We stole the turnips!'

'But how do you do it, without unlocking the door?' said the old woman.

But they only laughed and laughed, and wouldn't tell her.

'Oh, you can laugh,' said the old woman. 'But I'm the one who's in trouble when turnips fly off in the middle of the night.'

'Never mind, never mind,' cried the children. 'We'll pay for the turnips.'

'That's what you said last time,' said the old woman. 'But that tablecloth of yours, it was fine yesterday, but I didn't get a thing out of it this morning!'

The children stopped laughing, and stared. Then they began to talk to each other, and the sound again was like starlings on rooftops, and the old woman couldn't tell what they were saying.

But at last they stopped chattering, and one of them said, 'Don't worry. We'll give you something better this time. We'll give you a goat.' And there behind the hut was a grey goat with a long grey beard, nibbling the grass.

'Tell him to sneeze,' shouted the children.

So the old woman did. And the goat began sneezing as if he'd never stop. And with every sneeze, showers of golden money exploded like bright fireworks in the air, and fell in the grass at her feet.

'That's enough,' cried the children. 'Tell him to stop. It will take us hours to sweep this lot up.'

So the woman said, 'Stop sneezing, goat.'

And the goat stopped sneezing, and stood there, quite exhausted.

The children walked through the shining coins, shuffling them about on their feet, kicking them into the air, and spinning them over the grass, as if they were dead leaves. They didn't care about money. And when they were tired of kicking them, they left them lying and took the old woman into their house and gave her something to eat.

A real breakfast, not a magic one – porridge, and scrambled eggs, and buttered toast, and a big pot of tea. It tasted delicious.

'What good children you are!' she said. And she ate it all, and licked the butter off her fingers, and picked up the toast crumbs as well as she could.

Then she took the goat away, and went off creakily singing.

'Did you beat those turnip-takers?' the old man shouted when she got home. But she showed him the goat. And when the goat began to sneeze money, and the golden coins flew through the air, the old man rushed after them picking them up, like a chick runs pecking up corn.

'Thank you, goat. Stop sneezing now,' said

the old woman. And the goat stood there, huffing and panting.

But the old man went on scrabbling for the gold pieces, and picked up every one. Then he never said 'Thank you'.

All he said was, 'I've had my supper. There's nothing for you.'

The old woman just tied the goat to a post where it could get at the green grass, and she lay down and fell asleep at once, for she was old, you remember, and had done a lot of walking. And the minute she was asleep, the old man untied the goat and hid it in the bushes. And he put one of the other goats there instead.

'They were my turnips,' he said, 'so it's my goat.'

Next morning, very early, he woke up the old woman again. 'Go and see how the turnips are getting on,' he shouted.

'But I haven't even had breakfast,' said the old woman, putting her stiff feet on the cold floor.

'There's no breakfast for you. The goat isn't sneezing any more money. So you can stop lying in bed, letting everyone steal my turnips.'

So the old woman went up the wobbly stairs, holding on with both hands, and when she got to the top, and looked at the turnips, she shook her head, and put her hand to her cheek, and shook her head again, for there were scarcely any turnips left at all.

And when she told the old man, he was so angry and he screamed so loud, that she unlocked the door as fast as she could and hobbled away. And at last she came to the little wooden hut.

This time the children were not inside at all. They were climbing and skipping and dancing all over the roof. And every single one was waving a turnip. As soon as they saw her coming, before she was close enough to speak a word, they called out, laughing, 'We stole the turnips!'

'Oh, I know you did,' said the old woman. 'But I'm the one that pays for it when turnips fly away in the middle of the night.'

'Last time! Last time!' shouted the children.

'I'm very glad to hear it,' said the old woman.

'And of course we'll pay for the turnips,' they shouted.

'Oh, of course,' said the old woman. 'Thank you very much. A tablecloth without any food. A goat that doesn't sneeze money. What will you give me now?'

And she smiled at them. She couldn't help it, because she liked the strange little children. Though really there was nothing for her to laugh at, poor dear.

The children stopped laughing. They stared at each other, and began to talk, like hundreds of birds in the evening, and the old woman couldn't tell what they were saying.

Then they ran into the hut, and when they came out, one of them had a whistle, a wooden one, the kind you play tunes on for people to dance.

'But I can't play a whistle!' said the old woman. 'Look at my fingers, swollen and bent this way and that with rheumatism. Anyway, I don't know how.'

'Never mind!' shouted the children. 'Just blow one note.' And they all crowded round, and giggled and nudged each other, and pushed with their elbows to get nearer to the old woman.

'Is she going to blow?' the ones at the back called out. 'Is she?' And they jumped up and down to see her.

And the ones near her jumped up and down too with excitement and delight, and shouted out, 'Yes! She is, she is! She *is* going to blow.'

So the old woman took a deep breath, and blew.

And before that one breath was blown out, three sticks had jumped out of the whistle, and were hitting her on the head, on the shoulders, on the arms, on the back – and no hands holding them. My, it hurt!

'Blow again!' shouted the children.

'Again!' cried the old woman. 'Once is bad enough!'

'Blow again!' shouted the children, laughing. 'Tell them to get back in the whistle!'

So the old woman did as they said, and the sticks got back and there was nothing to be seen but an ordinary wooden whistle.

'Take it home,' shouted the children. 'That'll pay for the turnips, and everything else too.'

'Perhaps it will,' said the old woman. 'But I can't see how. He certainly won't like it.'

But she thanked the children for the whistle, even though she was sore all over, and set off home again.

Once she turned back to look at the children, thinking they might be waving or smiling to her, but they were climbing about on the roof, standing on their hands or twirling on one leg, and taking no notice of her at all.

'They've forgotten about me already,' she said, and smiled to herself.

The old man was sitting in the kitchen, counting up the gold money. He started to shout the minute he saw her.

'What have they paid with this time!'

'A whistle!' she said.

'A whistle!' he screamed. 'That's worse than a tablecloth and a goat! Well, give it me! Give it me! They were my turnips, so it's my whistle!'

'Don't blow it!' she said.

'Don't give me orders,' said the old man furiously. 'I'll do what I like with my own whistle.' And he blew.

Immediately out jumped the three sticks, and they did beat that man. They wouldn't stop, hitting him here, hitting him there. He ran about trying to get away but they ran after him.

'Oh,' he began to cry. 'Oh! I'll tell you everything! The cloth's in the cupboard! And the goat's in the bushes! And I won't bother you any more about the turnips, I really promise!'

All this time, the woman was trying to get hold of the whistle, for she didn't want the old man to get beaten, nasty though he was; but he was rushing about so, she couldn't get near him. But at last she managed to grab him, and made him stand still. And she caught hold of the whistle.

Then she blew on it. 'Back in the whistle!' she commanded. And the sticks jumped back in the whistle immediately.

The old man said, 'Oh, you are a good, kind, old woman. I won't ever shout at you again.'

'That's all right,' said the old woman. And she went and got the goat out of the bushes, and made it sneeze a little money, to make sure it really was the right goat this time.

And she got the cloth out of the cupboard and she laid it on the table, and said, '*Turn inside out*,' just to make sure it was the right cloth this time. And when it came back with the finest dinner you can imagine, she said to the old man, 'You can have some too.' And they had it together, and not one cross word spoken.

But in the morning, oh dear, in the morning, the old man was back just the same as usual. As soon as he woke up, he shouted at the old woman, 'Get up at once, and see to those turnips!' Up the narrow twisting stairs went the poor, old woman, holding on with both hands. At the top of the house, she looked at the turnips and this time she smiled, and came down again saying, 'Not one gone. They told me they'd never do it again, and they've kept their promise.'

'I don't believe it,' shouted the old man. 'I don't believe it! I'll go and see for myself, and if they've taken one turnip, just one turnip, you'll be in trouble all right.'

And he started to climb the stairs.

But the stairs were steep and wobbly. And the old man wasn't used to them.

'You'll have to carry me up,' he shouted at the old woman.

'How can I do that?' she said. 'You're too heavy. Besides I have to hold on with both hands to get up myself.'

'Carry me up in the sack, like you did the earth,' said the old man. And he wouldn't have any arguments. He got in the sack, and she started to put the end of it between her teeth.

'Just don't ask me questions,' she said, 'and expect me to answer.'

Up she went, slowly and totteringly, holding on to the sides of the wobbly stairs, with the sack bulging with the old man, and the ends of the sack almost pulling out her teeth.

'Aren't we at the top yet?' he shouted from out of the sack.

She said nothing, just went on concentrating, one foot after the other.

'Are we at the top yet?' he shouted again.

Still she said nothing, just went on climbing.

'Can't you hear what I'm saying?' he shouted. 'You stupid, deaf, old woman! Are we at the top yet? Answer me at once, or you'll be in bad trouble!'

So the old woman opened her mouth to say, 'Nearly.'

But when she opened her mouth, out slipped the sack, and the sack and the old man in it fell bumpety, bumpety, bump to the bottom of the steep twisting stairs, and that was the end of him.

After that, the old woman lived by herself, and she was happier than she'd ever been. When she needed new clothes, or some paint for the house, or whatever it might be, she just asked the goat to sneeze a little money, and then she went to the town and bought whatever she needed.

When she was hungry, she asked the tablecloth to turn inside out. She never had any washing up to do because the tablecloth saw to that, and the cloth was always clean.

When people behaved badly to her, she gave them the whistle to blow, and that got rid of them quickly.

And when she was lonely, and wanted someone to talk to, she walked past the rollicking flowers and the sensible vegetables and through the dark wood, to play with the strange little children who were always glad to see her, and hugged her, and made her laugh again.

                      Snip snap snover
                      This tale's over

The Arguing Boy

Now this is a tale of a boy who argued. And this is the way *I* tell it.

Once upon a time there was a boy. And he had nine big sisters. And because there were nine of them and only one of him, he always argued.

One day he had argued so much with his nine big sisters that he decided to seek his fortune. His mammy made him sandwiches – jam butties, he called them – and she put them in a bag, and he tied them to a pole over his shoulder, which is what people do when they seek their fortune, and off he went.

The weather was terrible. It poured. The rain went straight down his collar, shot down his back, and came out of the bottom of his jeans. And his sandwiches turned into pudding. He walked along, squelch, squelch.

At last he came to a house. He decided to knock at the door and ask if he could sleep there, in the dry.

'Can I sleep in your house?' he said to the lady.

'I'm afraid you can't.'

'But I'm sopping wet,' he said, starting to argue.

'I know you are, you poor wee thing,' she said. 'But I haven't got room.'

'You've got plenty of room,' he said, arguing. 'You've got a whole house.'

'I'm afraid it's full of people. Tell you what, I'll give you some hot soup to make you feel better. There's plenty of that still cooking.'

'I don't want hot soup. I want to sleep here.' He was very rude.

Just then, the lady's husband put his head out of the door. 'Having trouble?' he said. 'Trying to sell you a vacuum cleaner, is he?'

'He wants to sleep here,' said the lady. 'I've told him we haven't got room.'

'I should say we have *not*,' said the man. 'We've a big party here, and people are sleeping everywhere.'

'They can't be *everywhere*. There must be *some* room,' said the boy, arguing away, moving his feet on the doorstep, squelch, squelch.

'There's no room at all,' said the man. 'But I'll tell you what – ' And here he started to whisper in the woman's ear.

'Oooh!' said the woman. 'He couldn't!'

'Yes I can!' said the boy. He was just arguing.

Whisper, whisper, went the man. 'Oooh! He'd be scared to death!' said the woman.

'I wouldn't!' said the boy, arguing again.

Whisper, whisper, went the man. And this time the woman said, 'Well, you can tell him. But don't blame me if the Bogey gets him.'

Then the man said to the boy, 'You see, it's like this. We've got a cottage next door. There's nobody in it because of the little Red Bogey.'

'The little Red Bogey? What's that?'

'Oh, he's a sort of hobgoblin. Very fierce and bad-tempered. Perhaps you'd better not go in.'

'I will,' said the boy.

'I thought you would,' said the man. And he gave him the key.

Inside the cottage it was dry, but very dusty. No one had cleaned there for years, because of the little Red Bogey.

The boy found a pile of firewood and lit a fire with some matches he found on a shelf. Soon it was blazing away. He took off his boots, spread his clothes on the floor to dry off, and lay down on the bed in the corner.

He was almost asleep in the flickering firelight and the steam coming up from his clothes and boots, when a voice said, 'I am coming!'

He didn't take much notice. After a moment, the voice said again, rather louder, 'I AM COMING!' He still took no notice.

But after another moment the voice fairly bawled, **'I AM COMING!'**

He sat up and shouted, 'If you're coming then COME, or else shut up!'

A pile of soot fell down from the chimney. Then two dead birds who had been stuck there goodness knows how long. Then a lumpy red foot reached down, then a second one, then the rest of the two lumpy legs, then a lumpy, bumpy, frumpy-looking little red man came scrabbling down the bricks, and jumped right across the fire into the room.

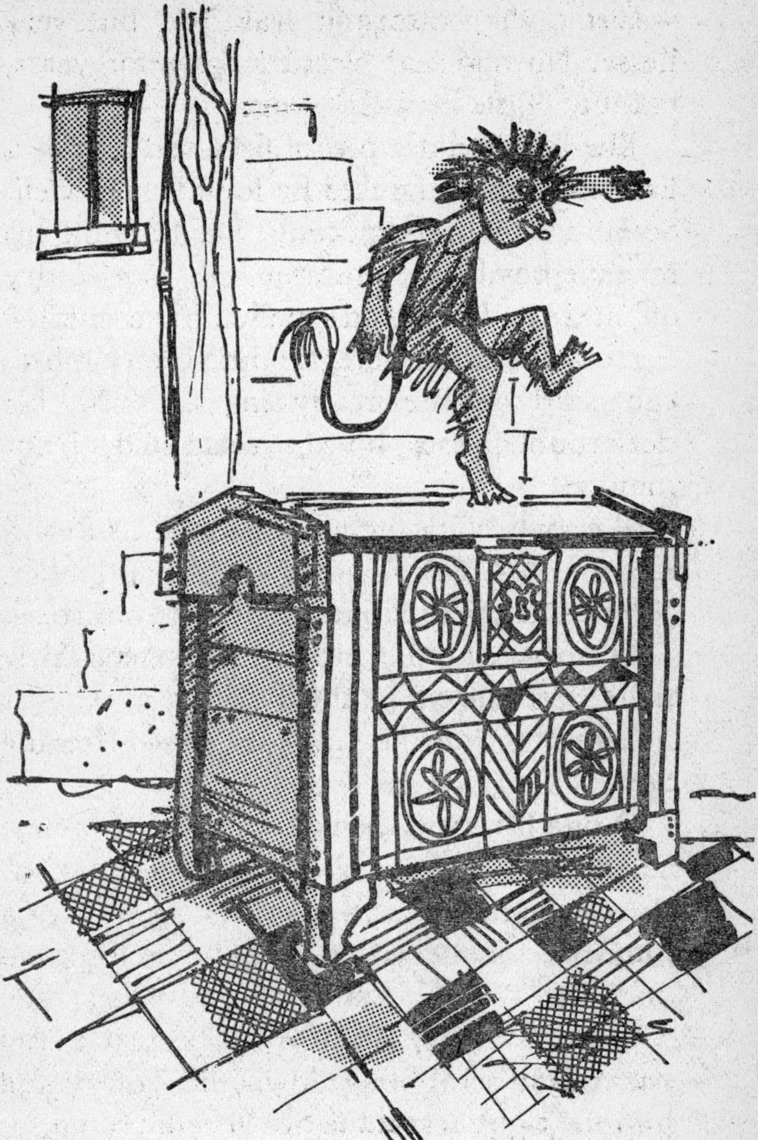

'Well, what a shrimp!' said the boy. 'The noise you were making, I thought you were a giant at least!'

'Don't you talk to me like that!' said the little man. 'I'm the Red Bogey.'

'I don't care if you're a pink cauliflower,' said the boy.

The little man strode to the door and flung it open. Two men were standing there, one on each side, and they really *were* giants. 'We've got trouble here,' he said. 'Arguing boy. I may be needing you.'

The first one saluted. 'Just give us a call, sir.'

'We'll chop him in pieces,' said the second.

'Right,' said the little Red Bogey. 'Stay there.' And he closed the door again.

'Now are you frightened?' he said to the boy.

'Not a bit,' said the boy.

The little Red Bogey scowled at him, then strode into the kitchen. 'Follow me!' he shouted.

'Why should I?' said the boy.

'You'll be sorry if you don't,' said the little Red Bogey.

'Who says so?' said the boy.

'You'll be sorry if you don't,' said the little Red Bogey, grinding his teeth and swishing his tail, 'because I am going to show you something very interesting indeed, and you will be very sorry if you miss it.'

The boy thought a minute or two, then followed him. 'I *might* come,' he said.

The little Red Bogey pulled open a trap-door in the kitchen floor. Underneath were stairs leading to the cellar. 'Get down there!' he said.

'Why should I?' said the boy.

'You're frightened of the dark, I bet,' said the little Red Bogey.

'I am *not*!' said the boy. And he went down.

At the bottom was an enormous chest. 'Open it!' said the little Red Bogey.

'Open it yourself!' said the boy.

'Oh, you really are a nuisance,' said the little Red Bogey. 'You really make me so tired.' And he started to pull at the lid. He was very small, and the chest was very big, and the lid very heavy by the look of it. But the boy didn't help him at all.

The little Red Bogey kicked the chest, and pulled it, and shouted at the boy, 'You're as bad as I am!'

In the end, after a particularly heavy thump, the lid flew open and there was a pile of golden coins inside, flashing and glittering.

'Here! Who does that belong to?' said the boy.

'It's mine. All mine,' said the little Red Bogey.

'I don't believe you,' said the boy.

'Yes, it is!' shouted the little Red Bogey. 'But I'm giving it to you, if you'll only give me a chance. I'm giving it to you and the people next door.'

'No, you're not', said the boy. 'Where did you get it?'

'I stole it.'

'Then give it back.'

'I can't give it back. It was hundreds of years ago. I've been trying to give it away over and over again, but everyone runs away from me.'

'Well, it's nothing to do with me. I don't want it,' said the boy, and started to go up the steps again.

'It's a rule!' shouted the little Red Bogey. 'I stole it from a human being. So I've got to give it back to a human being. That's the rule!'

The boy stood still and thought, while the little Red Bogey waved his tail like an angry cat.

Then he said, 'Oh well, if there's a rule, that's different. All right, I'll take it.'

'Thank goodness for that,' said the little Red Bogey. 'Let me get away from you and have some peace.' And he dashed up the steps, and the boy came into the room just in time to see his red knobbly feet vanishing up the chimney.

'I wonder if the giants are still outside the door,' he said. But they'd gone too.

In the morning, the man and the woman from next door came round to see if he was all right. They were pleased to find him still there, and very surprised to hear about the money. Very pleased too.

The boy bought four tins of paint with some of his share, and painted the cottage yellow and white so that he could live there. Later he asked their daughter to marry him, and when she said no, he argued.

But she said, 'If you argue with me, I'll never speak to you again. Ask me again next year, without arguing in between.'

And the next year she said yes.

They had twelve children, six of them boys, six of them girls. And none of them ever argued, not even about how that chestful of money had got into the cottage in the first place.

Snip snap snover
That story's over

Uncle Bouki Goes Fishing

Now this is the tale of two men and a boat. And this is the way *I* tell it.

There was one time when Uncle Bouki and Clever Dick bought a boat together. A fishing boat.

Well, you know what Clever Dick is like. Uncle Bouki should really have had more sense than to do anything with Clever Dick. But of course, Uncle Bouki *doesn't* have any sense. Why, I bet you've got more sense in your one little finger than Uncle Bouki has in the whole lot of him.

Well, anyway, there they were, the two of them, with the new boat that they'd bought between them lying there on the shore. Uncle Bouki was stretched out with his eyes shut, thinking about the shoals of fish they'd catch with the boat, and the piles of money they'd get for the fish, and the donkeys and the houses he'd buy with the money – sweet dreams he was having.

Suddenly, he wondered what Clever Dick was doing. He opened his eyes. Clever Dick was squatting on his heels, painting something on the boat. *His* boat. *Uncle Bouki's* boat.

'Hey, what d'you think you're doing?' said Uncle Bouki.

'Just painting the name of the boat,' said Clever Dick, twirling the brush daintily. 'There. *Saint Peter*.' And he took a little bottle out of his pocket, and shook a few drops of rum over the name. 'Now it's properly christened,' he said.

Uncle Bouki thought a moment. 'Wait a minute, wait a minute,' he said. 'It's *my* boat, as much as yours, you know.' And he grabbed the brush from Clever Dick, and began painting at *his* end of the boat.

'*Saint John*,' he said. 'That's the name of *this* end. *And* I'll christen it too.' And he took a bottle out of his pocket, and scattered some drops over *his* end.

'Hm,' said Clever Dick. He stood up, and began to test the sail. He ran it up four times, to make sure it was working.

'Wait a minute!' said Uncle Bouki. 'It isn't *your* sail.' And he ran it up again – five times.

'Hm,' said Clever Dick again. 'Hm.'

Well, they took the boat out to sea, and spread the net for the fish.

The fish almost leapt in, and when the net was full, and ready to be pulled in, Clever Dick said, 'Don't you bother, Uncle Bouki. You take it easy. I'm boss here. I'll do it.'

'*You're* boss!' shouted Uncle Bouki. 'Just wait a minute. You're boss? *I'll* do it.' And he pulled it in, flopping with fish, and heavy as lead.

They threw it out again, to get another catch. And again, when it was flopping full, Clever Dick said, 'You rest, Uncle Bouki. I'm in charge. *I'll* do it.'

'Just wait a minute,' shouted Uncle Bouki. '*You're* in charge, are you? You've got another think coming. Sit down – I'll do it.'

And so it went on. And the net was very heavy, and Uncle Bouki was getting very tired. Clever Dick still looked smart and tidy like he always does, and just smiled in a reproachful way at Uncle Bouki.

At last it was time to turn the boat for home. But the wind wouldn't blow the sails, and the boat stood still.

'We'll have to use the oars,' said Clever Dick. 'Don't worry. I'm stronger than you. I'll do the rowing.'

'You're stronger than me?' shouted Uncle Bouki. 'Just wait a minute. Who d'you think you are! *I'll* do the rowing!' So he rowed them home.

They reached the shore, and landed all the fish. What a gleaming, silvery, slippery pile. They both looked at them, and Clever Dick said, 'How shall we share them out, do you think?'

'Why, one for you and one for me. One for you and one for me. And so on till they're all gone,' said Uncle Bouki.

'Well, I'll tell you what,' said Clever Dick. 'They look very small to me. Perhaps they'll be bigger tomorrow. You have all of them today, and I'll have all of them tomorrow.'

'Wait a minute, wait a minute,' said Uncle Bouki. 'I'm not silly. *You* have all of them today, and I'll have all of them tomorrow.'

So Clever Dick took all the fish.

The next day, Clever Dick started to run the sail up, to make sure it was working, but Uncle Bouki said, 'Leave that alone. I'll do it.'

And when Clever Dick said he'd haul in the net, Uncle Bouki said, 'Leave it alone. I'll do it.'

And when Clever Dick said he'd row them home, Uncle Bouki said, 'Leave it alone. I'll do it.' And – yes, you've guessed it – Clever Dick took all the fish home. (Well, Uncle Bouki told him to.)

They went on for days like that. How many kilos of fish Clever Dick took home, no one will ever know. How many Uncle Bouki took home we all know – none.

One day (you'll scarcely believe this) the net tore a little.

And when they got to the shore, Clever Dick said, 'Well, of course I know more about nets than you do, so I'll take the net home and my wife will mend it.'

And Uncle Bouki said at once, 'Who said you know more about nets than me? *I'll* take it home, and *my* wife will mend it.'

The days went by, and Uncle Bouki was so tired he could scarcely get up and go to the beach each morning. He got thinner and thinner, and hungrier and hungrier. He just couldn't understand what was happening. Clever Dick looked so spruce, so rested – *so fat*.

One day they had just brought in the catch, and Clever Dick had just said, 'Well, they're rather small today. You take them, and I'll wait till tomorrow,' and Uncle Bouki had just started to answer, 'Don't you tell *me* what to do. *You* take them ...'

And at that moment, he stopped. He stood by the boat, and he began to count on his fingers. 'Monday. Tuesday. Wednesday. Thursday.'

Clever Dick began very, very quietly to tiptoe backwards. He was almost at the top of the beach, when Uncle Bouki looked up, gave a tremendous roar, pulled his big knife out of his belt, and was after him.

Over the beach they ran, up the road, and on towards the market. Uncle Bouki was catching up. Clever Dick ran into the market, wedged himself into the crowd, bent down, and made a noise like a hen clucking.

'Cluck-cluck-cluck-cluck-*cluck*! Cluck-cluck-cluck-cluck-*cluck*!' But Uncle Bouki saw him, and kept after him.

He ran into the church, and joined in the singing. 'All things bright and beautiful ...' But Uncle Bouki saw him, and kept after him.

He ran out of the church at the back, and round the corner, whee! and tried to jump the wall. Too high, *much* too high.

He could hear Uncle Bouki's feet pounding along. There was a hole in the wall. He scrambled through. But he was fatter than usual from all that fish, and he stuck halfway.

Round the corner came Uncle Bouki, fast. No Clever Dick to be seem. Only somebody's bottom sticking out from a hole in the wall.

Uncle Bouki stopped. Very politely he went up to the bottom and said, 'Excuse me for troubling you, but did you see which way Clever Dick was going?'

'Can't tell you like this,' said the bottom, 'Give me a push, and then I will.'

So Uncle Bouki gave it a push, and the bottom whizzed through the wall, without telling Uncle Bouki anything.

Uncle Bouki went back to the shore. 'I shall have no more to do with Clever Dick,' he said, 'no matter how much he begs me.'

And he sawed the boat in half, and carried the half named *Saint John* further along the beach, and tied it up firmly.

'That's better,' he said. 'Now I shall fish for myself.'

Snip snap snover,
That tale's over.

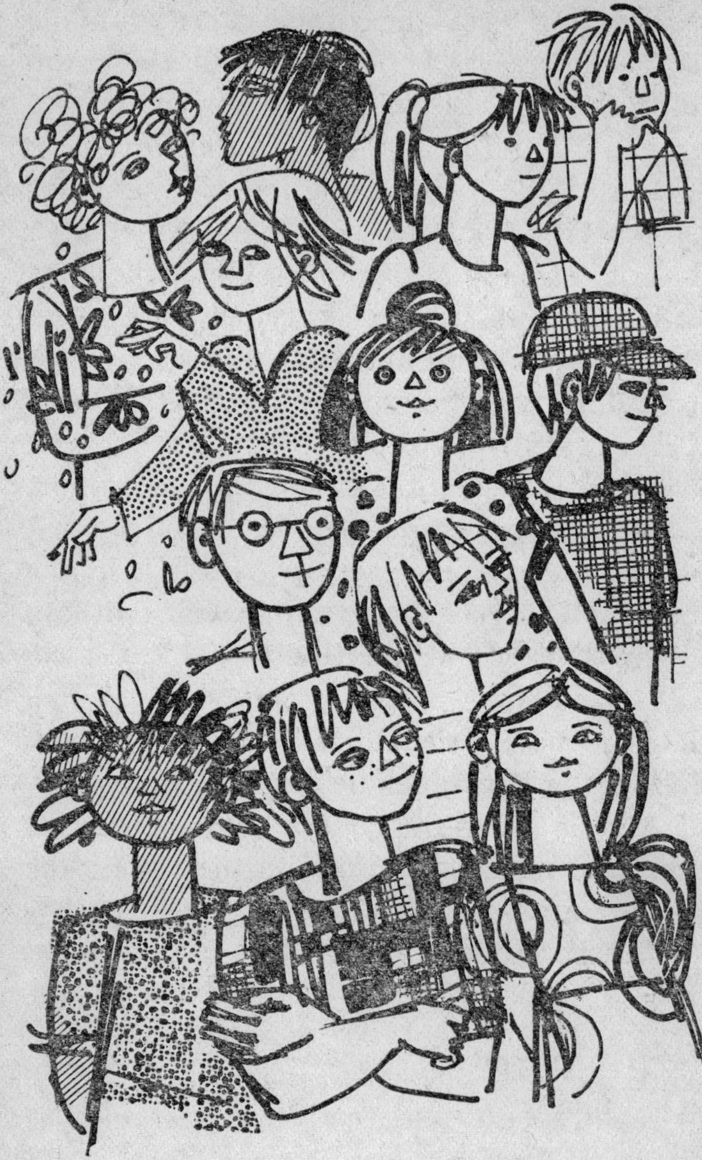

Number Twelve

Now this is a story of – *how many* people? ... Well, this is the way *I* tell it.

One day, twelve people went fishing. All friends.

There was Mandy and Sandy, and Jimmy and Timmy. That makes four. There was Poll and Moll, and Ted and Ned. That makes eight. And Bobby and Robby is ten, and Lindy and Cindy is twelve ... I *think*.

Hm, let me count them again. There was Lindy and Cindy and Bobby and Robby. That makes four. And Poll and Moll and Ted and Ned. That makes eight. And Mandy and Timmy is ten, and Sandy and Jimmy is twelve ... I *think*.

Well anyway, they all went fishing. And the sun shone, and the water of the river winked and flashed in the sun. Oh it was a glorious day for fishing!

Mandy caught a piece of wood.
Timmy caught a sausage tin.
Jimmy caught a boot.
Moll caught Cindy.
Poll caught a tree.
Ned caught the other side.
Cindy caught a man in a boat.
Ted caught Sandy.
Bobby caught a fantastic hat.

Robby caught a pram wheel.
Lindy caught Sandy.
Sandy caught herself.

Everyone caught something, so they were all very happy.

They went home talking and shouting and singing.

'I caught a shark in the sea!'
'I caught a thousand sharks!'
'I caught a whale in the sea!'
'I caught a million whales!'
'An octopus strangled me!'
'I strangled an octopus!'
'I'm Superman!'
'I'm Superwoman!'
'I nearly drowned!'
'*I* nearly drowned!'
'*We* nearly drowned *millions* of times!'

'How do you know if someone has drowned?' said Lindy.

'You just count,' said Ned, 'and if you're one short, then you know someone has drowned.'

They thought they had better make sure that no one had drowned. So they all got in a long line, and Ned stood in front of them, and walked down the line, counting.

'Lindy is one, Cindy is two, Mandy is three, Sandy is four, Jimmy is five, Timmy is six, Robby is seven, Bobby is eight, Poll is nine, Moll is ten, Ted is eleven, and - '

There was no one else there! Only eleven people! But there were twelve when they went out to fish.

They began to run about, looking for Number Twelve.

'Where are you, Number Twelve? Where are you?' But nobody answered.

After a bit, Poll said, 'Make a line again. I'll count.'

So they made a line again, and Poll counted.

'Ned is one and Ted is two. Sandy is three and Mandy is four. Jimmy is five and Timmy is six. Lindy is seven and Cindy is eight. Bobby is nine and Robby is ten. Moll is eleven and...'

There was no one else to count. Number Twelve had gone!

They were really scared. They ran about looking for Number Twelve. Somebody else counted, and then somebody else. But whoever counted – and in the end, *everybody* had a turn at counting – it always came to the same, eleven. No Number Twelve. But they certainly had Number Twelve when they started out.

'Somebody's drowned!' they cried to each other. 'Somebody's drowned!'

And they all ran back to the river, and ran along the bank, looking and calling and looking and calling, and back the way they came, looking and calling again.

But not a sign did they see of Number Twelve. So they began to cry, all of them.

While they were sitting in a heap, crying, a man came along.

'Whatever's the matter?' he said.

'We've lost Number Twelve, poor Number Twelve! Number Twelve's drowned,' they wailed.

'Really? Why do you say that?'

'We counted. We all counted. But there's no Number Twelve any more.'

'Now calm down,' he said (for the noise was tremendous). 'Just count again for me.'

So Cindy counted. Everyone got in a line, and Cindy walked along it, counting. And it came to eleven.

'Yes, you're right,' said the man. 'I see. I shall have to think very hard about this. You're rather lucky I came along, you know. I *think*, I really do *think*, that I *might* be able to find Number Twelve for you. But what will you give me if I do?'

'Oh, everything we've got, everything!' And they turned out their pockets on the spot, and gave him everything that was in them. They did want to see dear Number Twelve again.

'Right!' said the man. 'Stand in a line, everyone.' And he took a stick, and counted each one of them, and tapped each head with the stick as he counted.

'There's one. There's two. There's three. There's four. There's five. There's six. There's seven. There's eight. There's nine. There's ten. There's eleven.'

And when he got to twelve – because of course there *were* twelve of them when they were all together in one line – he gave that one an extra hard bonk on the head.

'THERE'S NUMBER TWELVE!' he shouted.

They were so excited! So pleased! So thankful! They all rushed up to Number Twelve.

'You're back! How lovely to see you! We thought we'd never find you again! Let me give you a hug! Let me give you a kiss! Where have you *been*? Then they all all of them shouted together, 'Yes, where have you *been*?'

And Number Twelve, who was still quite dazed from the thump, said, 'Me? I don't think I've been anywhere.'

'Don't be so silly. You *must* have been somewhere or we couldn't have found you,' they said. 'Wasn't it lucky we did?'

And they all went home, the twelve of them
... Or eleven ... Or was it thirteen? ... Hm.

Snip snap snover,
That tale's over.